OAK LEAVES 2024

RED OAK WRITING

OAK LEAVES 2024

Young Writers at Red Oak

We are proud of our young writers and the work they did during our week together at writing camp. In five short days, the pieces in this book emerged from idea to draft, from draft to workshopped piece. Participants learned that our best writing usually doesn't flow easily from our fingers the first time around, but--with hard work and a little help from our friends--it grows like flowers in a well-tended garden. We know the lessons learned at camp will serve our young people, both at the page and later in life. We hope you enjoy reading these excerpts and works-in-progress as much as our young writers did creating them!

Thank You!

Through monetary contributions, moral support, and other good deeds, many people come together to make Creative Writing Camp a memorable and enriching experience for our young people. We are grateful to all who have lifted up our writers in so many ways, including Joan Boyce, Autumn Green, Darlene Junker, Tom Malin, & Jennifer Rupp--and Judy Bridges, whose vision to nurture young people at the page started it all.

Contents

By Writers Entering Sixth
Through Eighth Grades

1

Nora Bolin

Diary of a Broken Girl

This is an excerpt from a story called *Diary of a Broken Girl* that I wrote at a Red Oak Creative Writing camp in the summer of 2024.

- Nora Bolin

A funeral. It takes a funeral to bring us closer together as a school. Pathetic. Everyone's in shock but no one is surprised. We all knew that, eventually, the bullying, the division, would cost someone their life. And yet, it never stopped. People just keep pushing, and poking, and prodding. That's the problem with the people around me. They keep pushing until it's gone too far. Until there's no turning back, no way to rewind. Until somebody feels so hopeless that they lose the will to live. They feel like no one would miss them. It feels like if you just died, the pain and suffering would stop.

I look around and take in the venue. There's a closed coffin at the front of the room and a picture of Emily, the girl who died, beside it. It must've been her senior school photo. The silence is crushing and the taste of salty tears is all around us. The room is extremely elaborate with delicate detailing on the walls and ceiling. This room should be used for a joyous occasion, not an event such as this.

I take in the masses of people in black, but I still feel numb. Like this is an out of body experience and that my soul has left my body. I'm not sad, not angry, I don't feel anything. I study peoples' faces, especially the bullies. Some look sad, but not really. It's just a facade. Others look genuinely guilty, like they know they played a role in all of this. And the worst of all are the bullies who show no emotion. They aren't sad or guilty. They genuinely don't care. It makes me sick.

I was never very close to Emily, but my older sister, Alyssa, was. Ever since my sister walked in the door on the first day of her freshman year, her and Emily have done everything together. Studying for exams, going to school dances, doing each other's makeup. They were supposed to be best friends forever. Now, she's an emotional wreck. She doesn't know what to do, who to be, where to go. There's a hole in her heart that I know all too well.

Emily's mom takes the podium wearing a long sleeved-black dress with a white lily in her hair. It appears that she attempted to do her makeup earlier, but has cried it all off. Her mascara is smeared, and a single tear rolls down her cheek as she attempts to compose herself. She then starts saying all the things people say to make death sound less horrible. Things like "she's in a better place now" or "she's looking down on us from heaven." Things people say because it's too hard to talk about what death actually is. The end of a life you can never get back.

The rest of the funeral goes by in a blur of tears and condolences until, soon enough, I'm back in the car with my parents and broken sister. I stare out the window while thinking about all the life Emily still had to live. This would've been the year of her high school prom. She never found love, learned to drive, or had a family. Never got to see her children grow up and never got to have grandchildren. Her life was only just beginning, and it ended in the blink of an eye. When we get home, we all go off to our own separate rooms, too emotionally exhausted to do anything else.

###

2

❦

Marisa Lovelace

Whisper in the Wind

There are two double doors that stand tall, at least twice my height. Lockwood opens the doors, and the room is extremely large. The sleeping quarters would be diminutive compared this. There's a large canopy bed nestled in the middle of the room, a deep maroon silk draped over the wood. To the left of the bed there's a large commode, clothing draped over the sides. The room, in general, is messy, things strewn around haphazardly.

"Excuss the mess. Zach is…hesitant to let me clean around here. Let me escort you to his office." Lockwood laughs, patting me on the back softly, guiding me to a small door in the corner of the room. He opens the door, and this room contrasts to the bedroom I was in originally. It's clean, organized. There's barely any decoration in the space. It's bland, desolate, miniscule. A desk made of a deep mahogany and a chair nestled close. And in that chair is someone, someone I can assume is Zach. He's sitting there, his head between his arms, asleep. He's hunched over the table, the small bit of hair that's peeking through his dark hood, messy. His ears are hidden beneath the hood as well, but I can see the sharp point of them, the difference in them from mine.

Lockwood sighs softly, resting his hand on his shoulder, shaking him softy. "Zach, he's here," he says. So I was correct; that is Zach. He groans as he wakes, head lifting from the desk slowly. Stress is evident on his face, dark bags underneath his eyes. It looks almost inapt for the rest of his healthy, youthful body.

"Hmm…" Zach groans, sitting up from the desk and rubbing at his weary eyes. He sniffles, rubbing his palms together as he looks up at me. I watch as he grimaces, scooting his chair a bit back for a bit more room from me. He seems disgusted by my appearance, by the dirt caked under my nails and the grease soaked into my hair. He seems to disdain the way I dress, what would be considered peasants' clothing to him.

"So, you're the one I have to work with?" he asks, an eyebrow raised as he looks me up and down.

I swallow thickly, the revulsion evidently clear in his gaze. I nod shyly, and watch as he sighs, running a hand over his face.

"Good lord, Lockwood, you sure *he's* the only one?" Zach asks, looking up at him with an angered expression.

"Yes. I'm sure, sir, and I would advise you to be a bit more considerate with him." Lockwood spits between clenched teeth. This seems to be the first time he's looked anything other than calm, experienced, any other emotion besides satisfaction. Zach doesn't respond physically, his eyes still burning a hole through me.

"Fine. Long story short, we're the same, in retrospect. You know how everyone went to some teacher this morning? Well, I'm yours. You and I both hold the ability to manifest darkness, shadow, umbra, whatever you'd like to call it. While the others learn to light candles and fill a glass with water...You'll be worjing with me, on...A few more drastic practices." Zach mumbles vaguely, clearly not wanting to elaborate on what 'drastic practices' are.

His eyes linger on my form, staring at the furrow in my brow, the uncertainty present in my body. I don't know why I'm here, what I'm fighting for, no one has informed me, or any of the others here anything. He clears his throat and turns to Lockwood, muttering something quietly that I can't hear. Lockwood nods curtly before heading out of the room with haste, shutting the door completely silently behind him.

"Were going to move you into a spare bedroom here in the south wing for the rest of your stay. It'll be more practical for both you and me, understand?" Zach asks. He sounds so annoyed, so vexed at the thought of spending more time with me, even though he's the one initiating such close proximity. I give a small, gentle nod, and he just stares with his brow furrowed in gentle confusion. "Do you not talk?" He scoffs, shaking his head softly. It's just now that I realized I haven't spoken a single word here.

"Yes, your majesty, I do..." I whisper, my head down to keep my voice as low as possible. He seems perplexed at my courtesy, as if I've done something wrong.

3

Abigail Mace

"The Advantages to Being Dead": An Excerpt

TRIGGER WARNING: This excerpt is about a teenage girl having a panic attack.

I can feel it again.

All over again.

His cold hands on my skin, a loud SMACK! The pain, fierce, bubbling and erupting through my face. My screaming echoing through the dining room.

Mother's screaming. Rosie's screaming.

The slamming of a door.

It was all happening.

All. Over. Again.

I couldn't breathe. I could still feel the way his words, his movements inflicted pain upon me. I could still hear the door closing, the way she dragged Rosie from me.

I could still remember the pain.

I couldn't breathe.

My eyes flew open and I felt the next scream already on my lips, but it died immediately. From head to toe, I was trembling, my wire bed shaking like an earthquake.

I jumped out of the bed, kicking off the thin wool blanket and stumbling to the bathroom. My head was pounding, my heart was racing, and my throat was as dry as sandpaper. I inwardly cursed at myself for being this stupid… Why did I have to have that nightmare? I had brought on my biggest fear: a panic attack.

I slammed the bathroom door shut, fumbling for the light switch, the fluorescent yellow glow making my headache grow. I clutched onto the granite bathroom counter, panting. I needed to calm down. Focus. My eyes roamed the bathroom, landing on a few stray waterdrops sliding down the metal shower head. I closed my eyes, sucking in a deep breath, but the moment I opened them, I was back there.

Back in that awful place, the cruel, sickening memories raining down on me.

I tried to keep the tears in but I just couldn't.

I just couldn't keep trying so I let them fall.

The teardrops streamed down my face and I was bathed in a cool sweat as I struggled to get the oxygen into my lungs. I could still hear it. Could still hear their words.

"Pathetic!"

"I'm leaving!"

"Weak!"

I felt my face, my fingers finding the tender spot on my jawline where wicked purple bruises were already starting to form. I couldn't take it anymore. I let a whimper escape through my quivering lips and I clutched my stomach, my head spinning. I wanted to die. I didn't want to be here anymore, though I knew I desperately needed it. My memories went back to that day when I was ten, when Mother slammed the door in Father's face, when Rosie packed her bags and left.

When they abandoned me.

When my whole life crumbled before my eyes.

I could still feel his hands as they struck me, over and over again. I could still feel the weight of her words as they crushed my heart, over and over again. My hands continued to shake and I swayed from side to side, crying my eyes out. I was allowing the anxiety to beat me. I wasn't trying to fight it.

I honestly couldn't help it.

I vomited, the sickness and terror taking over. My vision blurred with the crying and black spots appeared in front of me. I lost my grip on the counter and collapsed, smashing my head on the wall on my way down. I didn't care though, as the pain seared through my brain like a whiplash.

I was beyond anything physical.

I remained lying there, my side against the cold floor, the tears and snot crusted to my face as I breathed heavily. I could feel something warm and wet trickling down the side of my head. I closed my eyes, letting my thoughts drift back to memories that reminded me of this moment. Several times I had been in this position, on my own dining room floor, tears and blood flowing freely down my face after Father had beaten me.

I lifted my quaking fingers to my temple and they came back stained red. Sniffling, I clambered to my feet, leaning against the counter for support. I winced at my grotesque appearance. My eyes were puffy, red, and bloodshot, tear tracks traveling down my pale cheeks. My palms were clammy and coated in sweat, blood crusting to my head. My hair was tangled and damp while my bottom lip shook as I was on the verge of tears again.

I let out a slow breath and turned on my heel, silently opening the door and shutting it. I staggered to my bed, falling onto it with a loud *creak*. I fell asleep again, wandering back to the land where nightmares lived.

4

Charlotte Moran

CHARLOTTE MORAN

Life

When you think of life
You think of joy and happiness
But what of the darkness
Hiding just beyond where the light reaches
Life is joy, but also pain
Life is happy, but is also miserable

A life starts when we are young
And finishes when we move on
One day a baby is young and new
The next it is old
When you die, your life finishes
Right?

Life is about living
It is also about death
You are like an ant
Just trying to live your life

Before it is taken
Remember that before
Your shoe comes crashing down
On that little, insignificant ant

We are brought into this world
And we are also taken out
But that doesn't matter
What matters is the memories you made along the way.

One day your life is thriving,
The next is not.
It's just life after all.
But here's a secret: You can control whether it's good or bad.

When I think of life,
I think of memories, of happiness and beauty
But also think of the agony and the pain
Everyone, even the happiest,
Have that one little moment,
When they dealt with something that made them angry.

There's a saying:
Hurting someone is like throwing a rock in a lake.
You don't know how deep it goes, and sorry won't cut it if it's gone too deep.

Be careful during life.
You only live once.
So make memories count.
Make friends even if it's just for a moment
Because when you do move on,
You'll remember each moment that's precious.

The most unhappy are the ones who
Don't have a friend to turn to.
Who didn't make the most of their memories.
Who focus solely on the negatives, because it is what they have taught themselves to do
Even though some people think
Good memories are only positive,
What of the hidden suffering?
Some people think

Bad memories are only suffering.
Think of the contentment that came before.

Life's something that's meant to be enjoyed.
Not something that's meant to be just struggling.
All the memories, the beautiful and the terrible
Make up something beautiful. A life. Your life.

You're like the earth.
Your memories are rain drops
Without them the oceans wouldn't be full.
You wouldn't have positive and negative things to reflect on
To learn from

Life is about the good times
But is also about struggling to reach where you want to be
Every person has a certain
Darkness about them that's from something upsetting that happened that they regret
Many think its bad when they show it
But without it, we wouldn't learn
We wouldn't be ourselves.

Humans are unique
Whether at birth, if one baby cries but one does not
Or when we get older, if one remembers but one does not
You are unique. Your life is unique.
Don't spend it living someone else's

That's life

5

Riya Patel

An excerpt of "The Day Of Destruction"

"Kaboom!", "Kaboom!" I was on the beach with my two best friends. First, my sister, Chloe, and Donna, my friend that I work with in the factory. Donna and I had met after we were constantly assigned to the same job at the factory. We were walking along the sandy beach, little pebbles stuck in our toes, grainy sand crunching under our feet, with not any cautions of what was about to happen. Why? Within 5 minutes, everything around us turned black.

PRESENT DAY: (December 7th, 1941)
CrUnCh. The hot sand crackled beneath our feet as we set down the picnic basket and laid out our towels. Donna, Chloe, and I were going to spend a day at the beach. It was Sunday, so we didn't have any factory work to be done.. I checked my pocket watch. It read, 7:22 AM. Dad said we have to be back from the beach at 9. I would definitely make most of the 1 ½ hours we had.

I tied my disheveled brown hair up into a messy bun and dove in the water. "Race to the nearest palm tree!!" I shouted to Donna and Chloe.

Since I got a head start, I beat them by a mile. I touched the palm tree to secure my win. It was rough and a chocolate brown color. All of a sudden, I saw lots of planes flying low, but I didn't really think about it because there are planes EVERYWHERE. We continued to play by the beach, and then at 7:43, we took a break to get water and laid by our stuff.

"Hey!" Donna untied her knotty crimson hair. "Do you see those planes? They are super low. It doesn't look normal..."

Chloe nodded. "Yeah.... That does look really weird..... What should we do"

I checked my pocket watch. It read 7:48. Donna had no time to respond to Chloe because this is where it all started

KABOOM! Rat-tat-tat-tat. The sounds of bombs shattering onto our soil filled the air. I heard a loud scream. I think it was me. Suddenly, everyone around me, lifeguards, other children, and parents started taking cover. As the responsible older sister, I had to take action.

"Ahh!! CHLOE, DONNA GET OVER HERE!!! WE ARE UNDER AN ATTACK!"

They bolted towards me like I was a pot of gold in the open, ready to get taken.

Donna ran under the sea of palm trees to prevent herself from getting hit. I followed. "Wait!!! Juliet, Donna!!! Should I come with you or what should I do???!" Chloe cried.

Frantic, I screamed. "SAVE YOURSELF!! Come by us, OR GO UNDER A CHAIR. Just... DON'T go by the water" Chloe's blue eyes darkened with fiery. The tide was getting more aggressive and higher each time the place where the sand meets the water got bombarded with bullets. I coughed and coughed, and now could no longer see Chloe. I squeezed on to Donna, only to save myself.

"We gotta get home! What WILL WE tell your dad!??? Also, WHERE'S Chloe???!" Donna screamed, clearly alarmed.

Everything was covered in smoke. All of the palm trees were no longer green. They had all turned black. In fact, a few palm trees that I faintly spotted in the distance had fallen over. Everything was destroyed. Donna and I wrapped our arms around our necks to protect ourselves. All of a sudden, I heard a voice, and a hand.

"Juliet, is that you. Donna?!!" Realization hit me. It was Chloe.

"YES, HOLD ON TO ME AND PROTECT YOUR NECK LIKE DAD TAUGHT US!!!!!!!!!!!!!!"

Thankfully we had all reunited in the last 20 minutes, because all of a sudden, there was a shower of shells. BAM BAM WAM BAM BAM.

Lifeguards on the beach came to our support by using their megaphone. "We have clarified that we are under attack by the Japanese. We are sending the military out, so stay calm, take cover, and stay safe. LOCAL TIME IS 8:43 AM"

After what seemed like 5 minutes, the smoke seemed to clear out. I looked around. My light blue swimsuit had turned black, as my towel and all of the food in the picnic basket. Chloe was coughing trying to aerate her lungs, and Donna dove in the water.

6

Juliana Wooten

Unveiled

My feet dangle freely over the edge of a cliff. I don't know where I am or why I am here, but the feeling of freedom is overwhelming. I stare at the Sun for a moment, just for the sake of it, but oddly, it doesn't hurt my eyes. A weird sensation creeps up my spine - like someone is watching me, so I turn around. Then I see her. Haloed in sunlight, a woman with warm brown eyes, long blonde hair, and a calm smile stares back at me. I swing my legs onto the ledge, never taking my eyes off hers. As I rise, she takes a couple cautious steps in my direction. She takes a few more steps, moving into a leisurely walk. Her pace quickens until she is running at me, arms stretched out. Tears fill my eyes as my mother wraps me in a hug, filling my chest with warmth. Suddenly, I'm falling with my mother left above. She calls my name, reaching for me, but our time is up.

- - - - - - - - - - -

My eyes snap open. I am lying on the floor next to my bed, tangled up in my lilac blue duvet. A knock sounds at my bedroom door and it creaks open to reveal a young woman with short brown hair and bright blue eyes.

"Morning, sweetheart," Delilah coos, "Time to get up and get ready for school!" I smile at my adoptive mom and I scoot out of the mess of covers, before throwing them up onto my bed in a heap. Delilah strides over to fix them, spreading them across my mattress and tucking them in.

Her eyes rove over my ragged appearance, "You sleep okay?"

"Yeah," I lie, throwing pillows and stuffed animals back up onto my bed.

"Tessa," Delilah folds her arms, "Did you sleep okay?" I give her my most convincing fake smile and nod.

Her face softens, "Breakfast is ready."

"Thanks Delilah," I say. She gives me a curt nod and heads back into the hallway, closing the door behind her. I change into jeans and a long-sleeve floral shirt. I add my mother's necklace to the outfit: a gold rose with a ruby in the center at the end of a long chain. I head into my bathroom and brush my snarly blonde hair, before tying it into two long braids. In the mirror, I stare at the dark rings under my hazel eyes for a few seconds, wondering if Charlotte would notice. The weirdo would put me in therapy just for sleep deprivation. I laugh at the thought.

7

Books We LOVE!

Refugee by Alan Gratz
Where the Crawdads Sing by Delia Owens
The Hunger Games series by Suzanne Collins
The *Harry Potter* series by J.K. Rowling
Room by Emma Donoghue
The *Five Kingdoms* series by Brandon Mull
German Boy by Wolfgang W.E. Samuel
The New Apprentice by Michael Weber
To Kill A Mockingbird by Harper Lee
The Book Thief by Markus Zuzak
The Fault In Our Stars by John Green
Gregor the Overlander by Suzanne Collins
Iron Widow By Xiran Jay Zhao

By Writers Entering Ninth
Through Twelfth Grades

8

Helena Baxter

I'll Never Understand Growing Up

When I was younger I was the only girl in my grade who loved Star Wars,
I was more interested in playing pretend than I was in the real world, so I played Star Wars with some boys on my bus and loved every minute of it.
I could express myself through aliens and spaceships,
But that only lasted a little while,
Once I learned the boys liked disgusting jokes and seeing who could be stupider I stopped playing Star Wars and started talking to girls in my class instead,
Learned to play a version of pretend involving cats and magic.
I never knew how mean girls could be,
Or how many of them would do anything to make a joke at my expense to amuse one another regardless of how *I* felt,
How popularity is about who is *feared* most.
There were so many times I didn't understand I was being bullied because I couldn't imagine doing it myself,
So when I was kicked and sliced apart by their words I returned to my own world of magic and mystery,
Playing pretend, pretending I'm fine.

I was told it would get better as we got older,
Adults have this warped version of growing up in their heads,
They remember everything changing when they turned twenty-something,
And that's really comforting to say to a kid getting cyber bullied,
But all that changed was how unfairly us girls were treated compared to the boys,

How our biggest enemy wasn't each other anymore,
But our world and how it influenced us,
How many people told us that boys will be boys,
When I got detention I had to sit and think about what I did,
But when the boys got in trouble they watched Star Wars with the male teacher,
They looked so happy that I went to join them when I saw it,
But the teacher quickly turned it off and told me to go to lunch,
They didn't remember playing Star Wars when I asked what changed between us, but I knew what changed.
We grew up.
So instead of watching Star Wars, I wrote my little poems and stories down since there was no one to play pretend with anymore, while I suffered through detention the right way.

I used to play Star Wars with the boys,
Now I get nervous walking alone in the hallway,
Because one day they started saying inappropriate things,
Because one day they were told by men with podcasts that harassing their female classmates was a-okay because we're just dumb women,
In this case,
Dumb women who get better grades than them,
Who volunteer more than them,
Who work harder than them,
Who learned to play pretend in their own heads and call it a Novel.

So when they started acting civil,
Starting being the bare minimum level of kind they could,
I told my Mom,
And we celebrated with our favorite show and popcorn,
And while we watched I told the characters on the screen that it would get better when they're older,
Because everything changed in eighth grade,
Even though it went back the next day.

Even though they are cruel and disrespectful of me,
I cried the day I heard the number of them that planned to join the military,
Because while I know they will probably be fine,
I went to preschool with them,
And now I feel bad about not wanting them to die,
No matter how small a chance that is.
Because they are cruel and mean and hurt me and my friend when we were walking down the hall,

Because we dress in converse and anime sweatshirts and dyed our hair,
Instead of wearing shorts and a tank top we would be made fun of for wearing anyway.

I'll never understand why I feel a connection to my friends from preschool after they call us slurs,
Never understand why I was villainized because I didn't find them attractive,
But they're celebrated for commenting on my body,
Celebrated for touching people who don't want to be touched,
I'll never understand why my 8th grade science teacher was the only one to ever fight for them to be punished,
But they weren't,
Because they "just" touched my hair,
Just "accidentally" kicked me because it was "crowded",
But when I defend myself *I* get punished.
I will never understand why my peers find that cruelty attractive,
Never understand why some girls have pushed me into "having crushes" since we were eight,
Then turn around and make fun of me for it,
Or why *they* get crushes on cowards who pray on their classmates because they're upset about their test score,
When I got an A.
I'll never get how kids who used to be so similar became so different.
I still care about the little girls who learned to play pretend during recess when we were away from the peer pressure and expectations.
Even if I haven't seen them in years, because we were all forced to cope with "growing up" differenty.

But most of all,
I will never understand why growing up is supposed to be this magical fix for all my problems,
How this magical "fix" is turning kindergarteners who play every version of pretend into monsters to be feared and survivors to be pittied.
I don't understand how people think growing up will heal all our wounds,
Because so far growing up has only dug them deeper while our imaginations tried to support our creativity in a new and unforgiving world of reality.74

9

Sophia Beaudoin

The Lamp

I was five years old on the Christmas morning when, at exactly 7 am, I raced downstairs, tearing open the wrapping paper of present after present until one made me stop. Underneath the red and gold wrapping paper was a present shaped like something I would've never expected to find underneath the tree.

"Is this...a lamp?" I asked, confused.

"Just open it," my mom responded, turning to my dad with a smile as I joyfully tore the wrapping paper to shreds. The lamp I'd just opened had a raspberry pink shade with a mirrored base in which I could see the excited reflections of my parents' faces. Confused, I turned to them and they explained that this was my present since I'd accidentally broken an old lamp in the months prior. They remembered how I'd felt so guilty that I'd stayed in my room all day and figured that giving me the lamp would help assuage some of that guilt. Happy with their response, I let my dad help me set up the lamp in my room and he says that he can still remember the way my face lit up when the lamp flickered on for the first time.

I was eight years old when the nightmares started. I'd wake up every night to visions of my family and friends being held hostage by nameless monsters with nothing I could do to save them, clutching my bedsheets for comfort, nearly hysterical as tears streamed down my cheeks. My parents would come running, sitting with me to console me late into the night until they realized that they were just dreams. Then they stopped coming, and I was forced to turn to the soothing glow of my lamp as I picked up a book I'd just learned how to read, hoping that the reassuring words of *Charlotte's Web* would be enough to calm my racing heart, the lamp casting a quiet, uplifting glow over me all the while.

I was ten years old when I had my first panic attack, my breaths heaving in and out of my body as my heart rate sped faster and faster, silent sobs escaping me as I pictured the disappointment spreading across my parents' faces at the sight of one of my many cans of paint spilled across my expensive new desktop. It wasn't until I'd calmed down that I realized that some of the paint had splattered across my lamp too, staining its raspberry shade cherry red no matter how many times I tried to scrub it out in the following days.

I was fourteen years old when I tried to run away, to end it all after hearing that my best friends had been talking bad about me behind my back. They ghosted me when I found out. Not knowing how long this had been happening and feeling a pang of emptiness, of loneliness in my gut I saw no alternative. I packed my things to go, too young to have any idea of where with the suffocating 3 am silence my only disguise. I heaved my backpack over my shoulder and crept across my bedroom, only to be cut short by a loud crash as I tripped over the lamp cord, shattering my lamp and causing my parents to come running. The broken lamp, the pain in my leg from falling, their shocked and disappointed expressions...it was all too much. I burst into tears, turning my parents' expressions to concerned ones as they gave me a big hug.

"It'll be okay," my mom reassured me as my dad scooped the broken pieces of the lamp into a container to be dealt with later.

"Am I going to be in big trouble?" I sniffled.

"Of course not. We love you," my dad affirmed and I felt my mom nod against me. I don't remember much from that night but I do remember them sitting there and holding me until my sobs subsided and I fell asleep.

I'm sixteen years old when I find the container, unaware at first of what these pieces belong to. As I glue them back together and they take the shape of a lamp, I start to remember and I'm unable to understand or explain why a small smile spreads across my face.

10

Sylvia James Buchan

bLoody teeth

use me once and then destroy
"i didn't want you anyway"
am i not what you thought i was?
does my brain get in the way?
white-trash sLut with something to prove
sweet young thing whose knees are bruised
it's not my fault that i'm this way
it's not my fault he wouldn't stay
don't you wanna be Like me?
don't you wanna be aLive?
don't you wanna be your own?
don't you wanna even try?
use me once and then destroy
my body's yours, my heart is mine
cut yourself on broken glass
choke to death on cherries and ash
am i not what you thought i was?
am i just not pretty enough?
he says i'm not good for anything
now it's getting hard to breathe
i'm not what you thought i was
and now you know i'm ugly inside
now, you won't Look at me
and now i'm the girL with bLoody teeth

but don't you wanna be Like me?
don't you wanna feel aLive?
and don't you wanna be your own?
don't you wanna even try...?

11

✦

Izzy Desisti

Behind the Knife
(an excerpt)

On the eve of 2031, my mother and father hosted a dangerous New Year's Eve party at our home. It was customary, at least of us upper-class elites, to hold such grand galas at every slightly reasonable convenience. New Years? A party! A birthday? A party! Even the smallest things such as the rising of a full moon warranted festivities that went all night, leaving drunken guests in their wake. I, of course, had seldom been interested in participating. I was a quiet child, more often engrossed in the paintings of the manor's museum than the powdered smoke of party drugs. Whilst my parents complained about their son not taking an interest in family affairs, I saw no need to. My parents had removed themselves from my life, and I had no reason to insert myself in theirs. At least, until this year.

I was 18 at the time, Soon enough, it would be my responsibility, as their only son, to take the business. At this particular New Year's dance, they set up shop at our coastal manor, and hosted it outside. The pillars surrounding the floor were adrape in vines with red and violet flowers, lanterns hanging in the eaves of the pavilion, and the usual stench of sweetened drugs hanging about the place like a fog. My mother had made sure to invite all the families with daughters and introduce them to me, her giggling with the mothers as we exchanged the customary dances.

After kissing the gloved hand of the sixth marriage candidate of the night, I make my way to the bar on the opposite side of the party. As I take a seat at the bar, I spot my uncle just a ways away, speaking with a clearly intoxicated man- an envoy from the French black market. The French had been one of our largest business rivals for quite some time, but Father had insisted we invite them as a peacemaking gesture. Clearly, it had ulterior motives as well. "He can't have been so careless as to get that drunk, though.." I muse, watching them.

"My thoughts exactly."

I startle a little, but manage not to jump. I look over. Sitting at the bar beside me is another young man, looking a similar age as me, perhaps 19 or 20. Though he looks a little out of place. He wears only a black suit and tie, hair blonde and curly, but tied back into a ponytail. He's one of the few people I see without a hint of makeup on, or god forbid lacking accessories. I frown irritably at him. "Are you lost?"

The man's eye twitches, and he holds up his hands, laughing companionably. "What, no, no, not at all... okay, a little." He smiles sheepishly. "I was trying to make my way to the bathroom from the sunrise terrace, but ended up here, instead."

"The sunrise terrace?" I echo, and look closer at him. "Why would you still be there? The festivities clearly moved here to the sunset terrace hours ago."

"Were they?" the man seems a bit concerned, but clears his throat. "I just happened to arrive a little late. I was on business. Y'know. Business." He winks.

"Ah," I say, thoroughly unamused. "You are aware you have no obligation to explain yourself, right?"

The man looks mildly flustered. "Ahem. Right."

We sit there for a moment, the man growing increasingly more awkward and fidgety. He's clearly hiding something, which means one of two things. Either he's just an idiot, or he was never trained in deception. How interesting.

The man clears his throat, as if to excuse himself, but I raise a hand. "Bartender," I say, without looking away. "Two drinks, please." I tap the counter twice, code in my family meaning, 'get the strongest for the guest.'

The bartender bows slightly. "Yes, Sir."

The man raises a brow and leans against the counter, as if trying to act like he never planned to leave. "Sir, eh? You own this place?"

"I will soon," I say with a thin smile.

As the drinks are delivered, I slide the stronger one toward the man. The man takes the drink graciously, and sips. His eye twitches mildly, and I suppress a smirk. Raising a glass, I say, "A toast to your fashionably late arrival..." I trail off and raise a brow.

"You need my name?" the man swallows and nods(again) with that ever present smile. "Right. It's Nico."

12

Mariessa Ferber

Poetry Collection

YULAN

Oh my sweet Magnolia
Does your heart know the meaning of contentment?
Your silk white petals
Blossom beneath the sun
Clustering into a gentle beauty
Known and cherished forevermore
When the sun rises in the East each dawn
Does the whole of your being glow
As if infused with the light of the Cosmos?
From seedling, to a flourishing acrylic of gentle life
My love, your hands connect our moments past
Our yearning, our grief, bittersweet
To a luminous future
Feathered with the inscriptions of culture and richness
As the mockingbirds burrow themselves
Into the flora of your southern sisters
Can you feel every fragment of life
Entranced by your sustinent roots
As their gentle souls abandon their fears
Taking solace under the shadows

Of your reaching arms
Your graceful past, filled with lore of beauty and hope
Lies within each seed
Carried by the wind, to places only God has
intended your meaning to flourish
In every pigment, your life flows through the blood of the earth
And the fabric of my body
Your serenity will heal the hearts
Of those without grounding

A ROMAN TRAGEDY

Sweat stains the beat down walls
Broken bodies of old brick bear their skin
Painting us all a portrait of times strength
And man's recklessness against its own innovation

Dim lights flicker overhead
Each dissipating body dragged under
By the intoxicating rhythm of the underground harmony

Bodies sway
Arms raise to the empty, perhaps in futile attempt to grasp something
Anything, tangible enough to anchor themselves to this fluid moment

In such cases as with music
Accompanied by the mindless cycle of deranged escapism and ecstasy
Is it possible to feel both everything and nothing
For nights cool air to wash you clean
And yet for your eyes to burn as the world spins faster around you

A witness to colors unimagined, in the absent eyes of an endless crowd
Could this be what it means to fall?
Is this what I have become?

Each line of poetry I have inscribed into my skin
Every sonnet and story of sin

Meticulously curated
To escent through my blood, into the lining of my very soul
Is flooded by the reminiscence of worldly intoxication
And reborn an abstract masterpiece
Of philosophical passion
Conceived against the simultaneous pursuit, and flee
From humanities most complex and dangerous canvas
Could a mosaic of such chaos and beauty
Truly be madness?

THROUGH GLASS PANES

A portrait of daylilies, opening themselves to the clouds
paints itself each Summer dawn
Bearing its bountiful nectar to each singing sparrow, and happily bumbling bee Dusted and
soft
Sunny yellow pollen
Dainty white moths circle each bloom
Bringing a wave of joy as fragile as each lilies petal

The pink flora of our childhood cherry tree
Slowly emerges within springs sweet season
Petals wash to the ground
delicately lying below the body of their mother
The aroma of flowering life
Poignant and regenerative
Carried through open arms
Taking root within my chest

When the moon glimmers beauty in a world of darkness
You beckon me to unveil you
To let its essence envelope each valley
The night had cradled within its arms
This curtain of darkness is not empty, to the contrary holds true
Burning stars and Silver haze hold the hand of the suns absent sister
This is the way God weaved the tapestry of the sky
Yin and yang

Sanctified sunlight paints my walls with a heavenly glow
Though golden lives shortly, and fades fast
She is reborn, again and again
Aligned with the spirit of dawn and dusk

Rain, the ongoing cycle
Purifying your witness
The sky and water, united as one
Forever falling
Never grounded

Through you I see all
And each revelation that passes through you
Changes me
Of each sight
And every story
Of starry nights
And morning glory

WISDOM

I look at those who know God
Those who look to the sky, and can hear His breath in the wind
Those who can feel his warmth within the suns cascade
And I feel horribly envious
It's poisonous green so far astray from the green of God's creation

I ache to know the foreign
To immerse myself into the depth of ancient scripture
I want to have poured over every epic and every story humanity has ever known
My soul reaches for the understanding of God and man alike
Of every possible branch of spirituality hidden within our very beings
I'm desperate for enlightenment, for understanding
To be able to contemplate the incomprehensible
To look out at the landscape ahead and understand it's lyricism completely
I want to delve into the symbolism each page has to offer

Of this ongoing story in which will continue long after I am gone

I must drown in the beauty of anything and everything
To lay my eyes on every frame of living and of earth
To have made a home within the art of it all
To put a piece of my soul into everything I do
So as I walk along these hidden paths I've created
I may recollect these luminescent fragments of myself and make them my muse
Capturing the essence of experience and potential alike
I want to have lived every possible life
To have ran laughing down every road I've ever come across
To bow myself to intricate footnotes and design of this complex and paradoxical world

The nature of my being aches for the secrets only the heavens can whisper in my ear
For my senses to transcend what I thought to be possible
And experience this earth as deep and as fully as my spirit may last
So at the end of one chapter
Holy winds may carry me further
To places only my soul has ever known

A VIEW FROM THE BUS STOP

The cows are out this morning
Maybe still asleep
Nestled together behind the barren branched tree
A distance away, stretching its limbs across the winter barred field
Smaller, weaker branches outstretching from their former
And more from them
Reaching furthermore until a sight to behold is made
A barren tree in all its glory
Still shading, still fruitful
Only in its rich air

Birds sing out melodious harmonies
The lyrics of which I do not know
Synchronizing with the swaying of leaves
Painted all shades of fresh, lively green

The birds are nestled within the clustered branched of families of like trees
Overlooking groves of lilacs and pinecone ridden brush

The skies gentle pink turns to blue
As the horizon births our warmth
Our light cascading over barren fields
Trees of broken lineages surround the road
Casting sun rays
Through communes of pine needles
and fallen petals

The air is fresh as new day
Let your spirit breath it in
May you it shape you
Don't let this light slip through your fingers
Let it etch itself into the fabric of your soul
This morning air is filled with the spirit of rejuvenation
It is a painting of hope

13

Evvie Lennon Boulier

The Only Sounds are Those of Furniture Being Moved

The only sounds Are those of furniture being moved, echoing from somewhere down the hall. Daniela watches blankly as someone moves past her, carrying a bookcase. A few minutes earlier, she was somewhere between excited and nervous, but the second she stepped into the lobby a wave of... *something* hit her out of nowhere.

Ugly, ugly, ugly. She can feel the word slam into her chest with her heart and she squeezes her hands so tight her joints creak. It's a ridiculous thought to have in such a lavish room, all plush carpets and polished wood. It even has one of those giant curved staircases that wraps from corner to corner, meeting at a giant round balcony.

Ugly, ugly, ugly. She waves the nonsense thought away, trying to focus on her surroundings.

Directly in front of Daniela, between where the staircases meet, a portrait stares right at her. It's a painting, judging from the ostentatious clothes and vivid color– and the way the subject seems just a little too perfect to be human.

Daniela drifts towards it, hoping to find a signature.

The subject is a young woman with clear skin, sharp features, and dramatically waved brown hair, pinned half-up with gemstones and gold clips. She's posed like royalty, spine straight, chin up, but the seriousness of her pose is broken by the wide, mischievous grin splitting her face, sharp as a knife. Sharp as her teeth.

Daniela wrinkles her brow as she gets closer. For some reason, the painter added a subtle point to each tooth. Weird.

Also weird– the way two sets of armors are posed in front of the painting: a few feet forward and tilted inwards, spears and swords crossed like they're protecting her.

When Daniela pokes her head under the little 'archway' of weapons, something catches the light. There's gold on the edge of the sword that faces the wall. She checks the spear. A matching gold line runs from the point all the way down the handle.

The subject smiles, pulling Daniela in. She reaches out to touch the frame and her hand sticks. She tries to pull back, but the muscles past her forearm don't respond.

Hungry gold creeps up her fingertips, gilding each crease of skin. The color bleeds into the polished cherry wall.

You'll see it, little girl, this place is just as ugly as the rest.

Is that thought hers? It's her voice, her mind, but the words distort and spin through her brain, leaving fatigue in their wake.

She turns her head, trying to find someone to help, but the lobby is empty. The gold spreads from her shoulder and across her throat.

There's silence in the lobby, then, from the portrait, the distinct sound of an exhale.

Daniela's arm is released from the frame, still shining. She flexes her hand, unnatural skin moving no problem.

The portait isn't beaming anymore, eyes wide and innocent, face neutral, but right before Daniela turns to run, the subject's lips twitch in a tiny, secret smile.

PROMPT(S): GLOW, SEEDLING, FEATHERED, FRAGMENT, EXOTIC, MAGENTA

A glow settles over the grove. A single vase sits on the ground, dead center, filled with a seedling suspended in water. Pale roots stretch and tumble out and over the thin ceramic, thin forms illuminated by the feathered light.

The roots move, tangling around the vase until it cracks in two. One fragment tips over and shatters, revealing an exotic mass of magenta feathers. The vibrant shade is practically blinding against the muted tones of the clearing.

14

Lydia Liegler

Ex. 1: The House as an Organ

The House as an Organ is a fascinating case study into how it feels to be under the skin of a wild animal, to be truly between, instead of within. Rather than treating the guest or home-owner as a morsel, meal, or something to be devoured or digested, (This is usually reserved for the mouth; See Ex. 3), the occupant is treated as a parasite or a genus of insect. They are treated the way you or I may treat a tapeworm, or simply a common irritant that grows within our bowels or stomach, gorging itself on the soft flesh of our insides. Or, a thing that moves between and/or underneath the layers of skin, bulging out in traveling or stationary pustules, lumps, or ribbons, if such thing resembles that of a worm

A house such as this treats its occupant as a pest, at best an irritant and at worst, outright hostile. If perceived as hostile, the house will try, not to remove the occupant, but to squash them entirely. The desired outcome in these sorts of houses is a swift and clean escape, politely, if effect can be achieved. Best avoid breaking windows, or harming the house in any way.

The flesh of these houses will be warm, and attempting to destroy walls or infrastructure (sledgehammer, or other renovation tools), will end with disastrous and frankly upsetting results. (NOTE: These houses can and will bleed. Treat the house as it is, made of flesh and blood. Cracks in the walls may drip, and if you reach your hand into the crevices, you may feel something hot, resembling the texture of a wet, fuzzy blanket. If your skin begins to burn, remove your hand immediately, if you'd like to keep it). Only attempt to destroy the house if it exhibits any of the following symptoms

1. Evidence of multiple consecutive deaths within the building, (ie. families in the span of up to a year, missing persons in the surrounding area, parties at the house from which guests do not return). Physical evidence may include:

a. Skeletons/bones/mangled remains

b. Blood/Organic matter that can be confirmed did not come from the house itself

c. Confirmed/provable outside evidence such as police reports/files or multiple reliable witnesses

2. Alarming/apparent signs of infection that cannot be attributed to the occupant's presence: Pus, mold, mildew. Carpets or other similarly cushioned furniture may have a damp, crumbling quality. If the occupant or any other guests begin to feel nauseous, lightheaded, dizzy, or fatigued, vacate the premises immediately.

3. Rot: Similar aspects to an infection, but in a much more advanced state of decay/deterioration. The area around a house that is rotting may be dried, parched, or otherwise devoid of life.. This is an indication that the house has become cancerous, like an old, shriveled tooth, rife with disease and riddled with holes.

If any of these symptoms occur within or around the house, remove yourself or any other occupants from the premises and create a plan. There is only one concrete and proven method to destroying a house such as this, and that is with fire. (NOTE: There is no way to "defeat" the house as an organ, as it is not a building with a mind of its own. It can either be left alone, or destroyed, but it is nigh impossible to live in peace within it. For houses that need "defeating," either through destruction or reconcilement, please see Ex. 4 The House as a Haunted, Ex. 6: The House as an Addiction, or Ex. 7: The House as a Labyrinth

15

Kai Ruiz

I'll Only Miss You A Little Bit

Send me down stairs in a laundry basket
Set napkins on fire
Tip ourselves upside down
Christmas night; wait for candles and the choir

Play with paste and make a mess
Play with clothes and silly dress

Push chairs back and pretend to blastoff
Climb the backyard trees
Take a swim, or bike, or fight
At least those days were free

Make blanket forts in grandma's basement
Hands full of chalk when we drew on the pavement

Make an alien house out of cardboard boxes
Get paint on our hands
Ask for ages for a cat
And play on the beach, getting full of sand

Tape in the bathroom to split the counter
Hide and seek, and I think I found her

Eighteen now, you're all grown up
Leaving me behind
Moving to a different state
Whatever happened to the time?

16

Olivia Thames

The Lost Light

As the dark ink filled the once-bright sky, the ocean rumbled. He looked through the only window of his frail tower made of stone and glass. Across from the window was a circle of shattered glass and broken hands. Even though the clock froze in time, its ticking never stopped. Tick. Tick. The gray-headed man's eyes darted from the storm to the clock.

"What are you looking at?" he asked, addressing the clock. The shards of glass, now with eyes, blinked slowly. The hands that had once pointed to seven and four now formed a frown and spoke, "Just a lost man, hoping to escape insanity."

Albert sighed and turned his gaze to the shore. Clouds rolled in like a bowling ball ready to strike his lighthouse pin. The clouds matched the heavy black coat he had worn for years. Rocks clashed with the turbulent waves, and the once-grand stone bridge lay in ruins, much like the town he had once called home. The clock rolled its eyes at the delusional man.

"The town is gone, Albert," the clock said, "and soon you will be too." It blinked as Albert's mind wandered to memories of the flower-filled, cobblestone city and the lighthouse that had been his home. Shaking the thoughts away, Albert asked, "How long has it been since the last storm?"

The clock, weary of Albert's confusion, replied, "I am just as broken as you." A crash of waves struck the lighthouse, shaking the floorboards. Albert stumbled and steadied himself on the metal bed frame, realizing the disarray of his living conditions. Stacks of brown-crusted rectangles were piled haphazardly. He approached them and saw they were books, spines upon spines stacked together. He turned to the clock for a comment on his poor health and memory, but the clock's eyes dissolved into the cracked glass, reverting to its broken state. Tick. Tick.

As Albert approached the heap, the titles on the spines began to glow. He squinted to read them: "Abandonment," "Hopelessness," "Disappointment." The words echoed in his mind. Suddenly, letters started peeling off the spines, glowing fiercely. Abandoned. Hopeless. Disappointment. The pounding of Albert's heart matched the rising volume of the words. Tick. Tick. The words seeped into his mind.

He reached out to grasp the ancient rectangles, knocking the floating letters to the ground. Albert grabbed as many books as he could and began stomping toward his window, the only glimpse of sanity left. He leaned out, looking at the deadly waves crashing into the rocks below him. He thrust the books out of his home, one by one, their fading light swallowed by the ocean. As the last volume disappeared, a blinding light pierced the darkness.

Instead of feeling emptiness, cool drops of water soaked his skin. Disappointment filled his face as he opened his eyes to the rain cleansing the insanity from his mind. Tick. Tick.

Albert looked back at the clock and noticed a new feature where the books had been: an oval frame with a circle in the middle. He had never seen it before. "How could you not know?" he asked. The clock, blinking faster in frustration, replied, "It's a door, your escape."

The storm intensified. Lightning struck, and thunder roared, warning Albert of what was to come. The clock urged, "Run now, Albert, while you still can!" Albert, now on his feet, struggled against the encroaching ink clouding his mind.

"I can't leave!" Albert screamed, filling not only his body but the world around him, driving him to his knees.

"Your time is running out!" the clock shouted. Helpless, Albert lay by the open window, taking in the view of the place he loved. Lightning pierced through the window, repeating a pattern he had seen countless times before. Tick. Tick. The waves whisked through the air like a conductor's baton, signaling the final note of a song. Dark water poured through the window, consuming the lighthouse.

As Albert lay engulfed by the dark water, panic surged through him. Struggling against the powerful ocean, he squeezed his eyes shut again. The ink that had invaded his mind returned, swirling with the murky depths around him. The water, rather than cleansing his insanity, sealed his fate. The lighthouse, once his sanctuary, became his watery tomb. As the storm raged on, the clock inside continued its steady ticking, detached from the tragedy unfolding within its walls. Water crashed against the lighthouse, drowning out any trace of life that remained.

17

Gabriella Wooten

Gone With the Tide

The sun was just beginning to rise, casting a soft, salmon-colored glow over the rugged coastline of dagger-like rocks. The light seemed to dance across the water, shimmering in a way that always reminded Benjamin Thornton of the mornings he'd spent fishing with his grandfather. Seagulls cried out as they wheeled in circles in the sky, little white bobs against a fading navy canvas. Their calls were sharp, echoing off the cliffs and adding to the sense of anticipation that hung in the cool, salt-tinged air. Below, the waves crashed rhythmically against the jagged rocks, white foam surfing along each swell. The sound was soothing, almost hypnotic, like the lullaby of the ocean.

Twelve-year-old Benjamin trudged up the winding path to his grandfather's fishing shack, his heart light and eager. He loved visiting his grandfather, Mr. Amos Thornton, who always had nameless stories about the sea and the days when the water was calm and the fishing was bountiful. As he walked, Benjamin would remember the countless times his grandfather had sat him on his knee, pointing out towards the horizon and telling him about the great ships that had once sailed these waters, carrying goods from lands so distant they seemed like fairy tales to the boy.
But this morning felt different- there was an eerie stillness in the air. The kind that made the hairs on the back of his neck stand on end, though he couldn't say why.

As Benjamin reached the top of the path, he paused, expecting to see his grandfather mending nets or preparing his fishing gear as he always did at this hour. The small, weather-beaten shack, with its splintering wood and lopsided room, stood silent. The wind, usually cool and bracing, was oddly still and cold, the usual sounds of the shoreline muted as if the world were holding its breath.

He called out, "Grandpa!" but his voice was swallowed by the whirling wind, the sound barely reaching past his own ears.

As Benjamin pushed open the creaking door, the familiar scent of old brine and old wood filled his nostrils. The kitchen, usually alive with the smell of fresh fish or the earthy scent of potatoes boiling on the stove was empty, lifeless. THe kitchen table, a rough-hewn piece of wood polished by years of use still bore the remnants of a half-finished meal. A loaf of dry fisherman's bread, just like the one his grandfather had taught him to make many times, sat torn open, the knife beside it smeared with curd. The curd had hardened, the edges curling up and yellowing, a stark contrast to the fresh, creamy spread that usually adorned their meals. Beside it, a soup bowl sat, the lingering aroma of fish chowder faint but still present. The spoon rested inside the bowl, handle tilted to the side.

The sink was piled high with unwashed dishes, a greasy pan on top still bearing the crusted remnants of last night's dinner. The smell of stale food mixed with the saltiness of the sea, creating an unsettling aroma that made Benjamin's stomach churn.

In the corner, the wood-burning stove was cold, its blackened door slightly ajar. A pot of water, once hot for tea, now stood forgotten, sitting upon the stove's cold surface. A single cup, chipped and stained from years of use, sat on the counter, a few drops of tea staining the bottom. Benjamin remembered how his grandfather would let him sip from his cup, the tea strong and bitter, but it always made him feel like a grown-up. The cup had always been warm, a small comfort in the early morning chill, but now it was cold, lifeless.

The workspace, a small area near the window overlooking the sea, was a chaotic mess. Tools and fishing gear lay strewn across the workbench, tangled fishing lines draped over hooks, and a few nails scattered among the clutter. The old wooden chair, splintering with age, was askew. A stack of yellowed papers, usually meticulously arranged, were now crumpled and smudges, fanned out across the wooden planks.

Moving deeper into the shack, Benjamin found the bedroom in a similar state of disarray. The bed, an old iron frame with a saggy, spring-filled mattress, was left unmade. The quilt, hand-stitched by Benjamin's grandmother long before he was born, was bunched at the foot of the bed, the pattern of ships and anchors now faded, frayed and threadbare. The pillows were untouched, no dent visible from his grandfather's head.

18

Lucy Valentine

When the Tall Grass Falls

April twenty-fourth, 2016

Tonight the king has sent us out to look for any food, or survivors past town. Considering he was "only sending out his best men", there sure is a lot of people, and not just hunters which came as a surprise to me, the total seeming to be pushing fifty. This journal is for us to keep track of the days that pass, the kinds of life we find, and things of that nature. We have not yet found anything notable.

-R,M, *Chief of Hunters.*

May first, 2016

Seven days have passed so far, with only one form of life found by Sir Mateo while drinking water. We are unsure exactly what this is, But the scientists theorize that it is an advanced strand of mold that has been mutated by chemicals in an abandoned lab after the freeze. Nothing else to report, besides that Mary's son has been acting rather aggressive due to an unknown reason, further reports below.

-R,M, Chief of Hunters

The ill:Alex diaz

Date of birth:06/24/2007

Gender:Male

Symptoms: Aggression, sudden personality changes, loss of motor skills and poor coordination.

-Dr.Solace

May fifth, 2016.

Eleven days have gone by since the beginning of the mission. Many of the crew's protection is getting torn, and food is running extremely low. I am beginning to think we may need to turn back, but if I'm being totally honest I don't know if we can at this point. Snowfall has been getting heavier each day, so we cannot retrace our steps.

-R.M

May eighth, 2016.

I need to turn back. I need to go back to the kingdom. We need to. Alex was found dead this morning, just a week after contracting that supposed illness, infection, or whatever it was. Everybody has been quiet today, besides his mother who disappeared after finding the body.

None of us will survive this if we don't get out of this cursed forest. We'll either starve or freeze, possibly even succumb to the same conditions as sweet young Alex. My fingers are growing numb from the cold, so I may not write as often.

-R.M

May eleventh, 2016.

7 more patients have gotten the same symptoms as Alex, I'm growing extremely worried. Seeing how fast it killed him, I fear what will come of our group. I have decided to temporarily call this "VIRUS-1". Fortunately, after preforming an autopsy I have connected virus-G to the strand of mold mateo found on May first. The mold goes into your body through water, creeping into the brain. It begins to rot the frontal lobe, then the cerebellum. This appears to be highly contagious, as it infected ◇ of us within less than twenty days

-Dr. Solace

19

Leo Valentine

Release the Earth

As the sickness grew The Boy could see it, an image in his head – the disease clinging to his chest like mold, climbing his ribcage, growing as his organs decay. The mold feeding on his body in which every component has its own purpose, his cells working together to create a functioning organism, a perfect collection of parts creating a single working unit.

But the mold doesn't care about this unit, doesn't care about the God that meticulously designed it. The mold isn't motivated by God but by something else, a force, a force with no plan and no purpose and no meaning. But the mold loves life as much as anyone else and wants to grow, having no mercy for anything or anyone. The Boy is its father and the mold knows it was a mistake, it knows its father poisons himself just to rid himself of it. And the mold hates him for this so it seeps into his blood, flowing to his brain, eating away at his entire body. It no longer grows out of a desire to live but out of pure malice. And this hate infects the mold's body, cells of hate within cells of a cancer demolishing a young life.

The Boy knows what's happening in his body. When he closes his eyes he sees the mold and the hate and the disintegration of his body. This image is the only thing he can be certain of and it crushes his hope. But the vanquishing of his hope gives him comfort and security because hope is an uncertainty, a possibility. And now that his hope has been conquered he finally has certainty for the first time in his short life.

He doesn't know what will happen to his soul when he dies, but he knows what will happen to his body. The disease in him will cease its hate, but it has no soul so it will just wither away. And his face will become a scrap, as will the heart that so desperately fought to keep him alive and the brain that put into motion everything he ever did.

And while the mold is consuming his body with contempt, the Earth will take him with tenderness, will cradle him and kiss every inch of his body until they are one. And after his body is assimilated he will hold his mother as she once held him and he will become a part of the phantasmic body of God. And The Boy realizes that he doesn't know what will happen to his soul, but

53

he knows that his body will give joy to the Earth. The Boy knows his purpose is to feed the dirt that he was borne from, the soil that will immortalize him. He doesn't know the meaning of life as a whole, but he knows his purpose as an individual which is the most one can hope to do in their lifetime

20

Books We LOVE!

From Campers Entering Grades 9-12

Romeo & Juliet by William Shakespeare
The Outsiders by S.E. Hinton
The Giver by Lois Lowry
Mysterious Skin by Scott Heim
The Tao of Pooh by Benjamin Hoff
The Sunset Limited by Cormac Mc Carthy
Aristotle and Dante Discover the Secrets of the Universe by Benjamin Alire Saenz
We Contain Multitudes by Sarah Henstra
East Of Eden by John Steinbeck
The Sound and the Fury by William Faulkner
Dune by Frank Herbert
The Alchemyst: The Secrets of the Immortal Nicholas Flamel by Michael Scott
Making Bombs For Hitler by Marsha Forchuk
We Were Liars by E. Lockhart
Girl In Pieces by Kathleen Glasgow
The Haunting of Hill House by Shirley Jackson
House of Hollow by Krystal Sutherland
'The Dash' (poem) by Linda Ellis
Luck of the Titanic by Stacey Lee
Unbroken: A World War II Story of Survival, Resilience, and Redemption by Laura Hillenbrand
The Bell Jar by Sylvia Plath
My Year of Rest and Relaxation by Ottessa Moshfegh
The Poisonwood Bible by Barbara Kingsolver
Dispatches From Puerto Nowhere: An American Story of Assimilation and Erasure by Robert Lopez

The *Murdle* series by G.T. Karber
'Bluebeard' (folktale) by Charles Perrault
'The Fitcher's Bird' (folktale) by The Brothers Grimm
House of Leaves by Mark Z. Danielewski
In Cold Blood by Truman Capote
Cannery Row by John Steinbeck
Hinds' Feet on High Places by Hannah Hurnard
Homegoing by Yaa Gyasi
The Family Arcana by Jedediah Berry
The Lover by Marguerite Duras

9 798330 412495